ALL THE FEELS

Volume 3: A Collection of Six Inspiring Short Stories

B. A. PAUL

Contents

Foreword

As I write this foreword, the year 2020 has yet to loosen its grip on the world's throat — we actually have three more months and a lot more chaos left, I'm afraid. From viruses, fires, floods, and droughts to social injustices and unjust politics, the year rages on.

We need a break.

A breath of fresh air.

An escape.

Somewhere to hide away and experience emotions other than fear and dread.

Perhaps you've come across this volume and the year is no longer 2020 (thank heavens!). Maybe your current year is 2030 or 3010.

No matter.

I imagine, wherever you are in time, dear reader, that you likely need a break, too.

My wish is that these stories will give you that break. A place to wonder and dream. A place to giggle a bit, hope a bit, and yeah… maybe cry a little.

But just a tiny bit…

Happy little eye leakage.

My hope is that these tales will give you a place to escape and to experience a wide range of , well, all the feels.

Happy reading!

B. A. Paul

Optimists and Pasta Mixes

Misunderstood and disgruntled, young Jody is ready to bolt from all she knows —but she's broke. She has no idea her part-time gig in a pasta truck will turn her pessimistic view of the world upside down.

"And why do you feel this job will be a good fit, Miss Jody Sparks?" The rather rotund, balding man behind the overflowing desk chews the end of his ballpoint pen, leans back and looks at me. He speaks over the rattling air conditioner someone had cut a hole through the paneled wall for. The unit does little more than blow around the stale, greasy aroma of food truck lunch remnants.

His question throws me. I have no clue why I'll be a good fit. I need money. Is that fit enough?

"Well, Mr. Farley, I—"

"Ed. You can call me Ed." He leans forward.

This isn't awkward at all. "Well, Ed. I'll show up." My voice elevates an octave on the word "up."

"Is that a question or a statement? 'I'll show up.'"

I can't imagine a plethora of warm, upright bodies ready and willing to tackle the ins and outs of street truck food service. "You have an opening, and I need a job. And I will show up. At least until I get enough cash to fund my great escape." There. Maybe that's what he wants.

"That, Jody, is honesty. Which is more than the last two new hires had when they took off with Miss Gloria's tip jar at the end of a very busy business day." He leans further across the messy desktop, knocking folders and pens off the side. "And everyone knows Miss Gloria's customers tip the best." He winks.

Ed creeps me out. The office in the mobile command center creeps me out. My life creeps me out. And I want out. Out of all of it. Away from my nagging aunt—god bless her heart for taking me in, but for crying out loud, I need my space. Away from the neighborhood where everyone knows what a screw-up Miss Jody Sparks has become. Out of it all to start again somewhere else.

Big city life is a joke. At least in my sunny California city. You'd think with such a dense populous that one could hide. Ha. City neighborhoods contain no different drama than what happens in suburbs. Only difference I can tell is that in the burbs people are all spread out from house to house divided by green yards. In our neighborhood, we stack the drama up tall and only separate it by thin walls of plaster and maybe—if you're lucky—brick. One house on top of another—and we smell all the dirty laundry on either side of our front door, above, and below.

And everyone knows my business.

And they all seemed to care so much. Not caring in the real caring way, but caring in the "Guess what Jody did this time?" way.

"Guess who Jody's hanging with now?"

"Guess what Jody's on now?"

That last one bugs me the most because I'm not *on* anything. Never have been.

I just think differently than everyone else would like. I don't see why 'everyone' is always worked up over me. I like the bad boys. I like the idea of escape. I hate school. Hate what life dealt me and my family. And I want away.

Cash is my ticket out. Away.

Away with Galvis, who is my only bright spot. He really gets me.

Mr. Ed hands me a manila folder of hire-on paperwork. This is my third time filling out such a packet. The first one Aunt Pam helped me with because what teenager knows the ins and outs of W2s and benefits and on and on with the mundane? That was at the burger joint a few blocks away. I'd met Galvis there on one of his lunch breaks. He'd promised me the moon—and delivered a sliver of it with his grunt-work construction job, but not quite enough to afford the grand escape we'd planned for weeks.

Galvis told me I could quit. Depend on him. So I did.

I'd miscalculated, but that wasn't Galvis's fault.

The second job packet had been from a convenience store. It got robbed—buddies of Galvis of all people. See how small my world is?—and Aunt Pam pitched such a fit that I quit—and the management there thought Jody *had* to have something to do with it. Now I'm in this office with Mr. Ed Farley and my third set of blank forms in four months.

And all this because Gal got canned down at the site for not showing up. Because he thought my mini-mart paycheck would cover our great escape and he could relax a little and lick his wounds when his "friends" got caught for stealing.

Galvis worked hard, he really did, though no one else would believe me about this, especially Aunt Pam. He deserves some time off. He'd showed up, faithfully obeying commands from the unfair project manager for over three months. The whole three months I've known Gal, he really has worked hard.

"I'll put you with Gloria. I think you'll make her a good partner. She usually sets up downtown, but this month, she's servicing a huge construction project on the west end. Lots of hungry men. Lots of tips."

I retrieve a pen from the floor and start the paperwork right there. If Mr. Ed's gonna rattle on, I'll at least get some of this out of the way. "What does her truck serve?"

"Pastas. All kinds. Different every day and dandy good, too." He leans back in his chair and rubs his bulging gut. One more pasta dish for him and he could aim his popping buttons as deadly projectiles. "Her own recipes and mixes. You'll get full-time hours."

"Well, Ed, that sounds dandy good." He likes my use of his corny vocabulary and beams. I can manipulate people pretty well when the situation calls for it. I hand him the completed paperwork and he tosses it onto a pile of similar folders in the corner of the floor.

"Grab your bag and pull that mop up out of your face. I'll take you to meet Gloria." He's all smiles. I'm all nerves. I rummage in my sack for a ponytail holder and fix my curly hair up tight in a knot. I'm not nervous about the job, but about whether I'll weather the impending boredom that was certain with this type of work and clock in every day. "The clock starts now, Miss Jody. Welcome to Farley's Food Service."

I thank him and follow him out of the office. One second closer to my goal. One dollar-bill tip at a time. If Gloria shares her tips. I'll have to figure out how that works. If that tip jar was worth taking off with, maybe this minimum wage gig could turn out to be something better. If I can keep my snark and attitude in check long enough not to get fired.

Long enough to dip my hand into the all-famed tip jar.

Or finally live up to everyone else's expectation of me and just take the dandy thing.

~

THREE HOURS IN. Three hours closer to skipping the 'hood and I'm ready to quit.

The glorious Gloria has smacked my butt three times. One love-pat per hour. All in good-hearted, grandmotherly encouragement, but totally inappropriate behavior for the workplace.

If you could call this stainless-steel kitchen on wheels a workplace.

I barely keep up with her. For an old gal, Gloria sure can move around this narrow mouse hole. Her teal-colored apron—and Ed gifted me with a matching one—is stained with yellows and reds. Her salt-and-pepper hair is cut short, a boy cut that suits the hot work environment. She wears a teal sweatband that circles her head above her ears, pushing a few strands of hair out in odd angles. Bright red reading glasses dangle onto her massive boobs from a black chain around her thick neck. Her lipstick matches the glasses.

The breeze wafts through the open service window, stirring the humidity rising from the boiling water with the dryer air blowing from an industrial fan hanging high in the corner of the truck. The pasta pots are large enough to cook three chihuahuas and a dachshund if you left the lids off. I'm not sure how the pots and her boobs all fit in this truck.

She put me in charge of salting the water and keeping the noodles stirred and un-sticky.

Before this, the only pasta I'd ever dealt with was Velveeta microwave cups. No muscles required for that meal.

"We start in earnest in an hour. You gotta be quicker." She hands me a white towel and nods at the water sloshing onto the counters. "Keep it dry. Fresh towels here. Dirty towels go there."

I moan. She hears it.

"You can do it, Jody. I know you can."

You don't know anything about me, is what I want to snap back at her, but I hold my tongue. In three hours, this woman dripped enough sunshine and roses that I want to vomit. I've never met anyone so happy to do such a miserable task.

As Gloria stirs and wipes and preps, she rattles on about how she misses her "loyals"—her regulars from near the courthouse and downtown boutique stores—but that she's making new fans here on the construction site. Good tippers too. Likely had wives or "gal" friends who didn't cook well for these poor men. Nor did their women have the foresight to pack an appropriate amount of carbs into their lunch buckets for the hard work the guys do all day. Building this ever-needed, earthquake-proof new development…

I stop listening to her.

I didn't want to look at the site too closely. There are tons of construction projects in this part of town, but with my small-'burg luck, this site is where Galvis had worked all those miserable weeks. I hope Rod the foreman isn't one of Gloria's fans. Hopefully Rod is on the keto diet and steers clear of all things noodles. Rodney was the one who'd fired Gal. I'd give him a piece of my mind and likely lose my crappy job in the process…

Gloria dumps another batch of penne into boiling water and hands me the ladle to stir. Stir. Wipe. Repeat. And we're just prepping. We've not had the first customer. No tips. Just minimum wage dollars.

"I'm so very glad that Ed decided to slot you with me. I think we'll get along just dandy." She takes my face in her fat hands. Just like a grandmother. "I know you'll do great, Jody."

And another slap on the butt cheek as she turns to the sauce prep. I see it coming, but there isn't enough room to dodge her hand without knocking boiling water onto us both.

I contemplate leaving right then, but I can't quit yet. If for no other reason than morbid curiosity over the tip jar.

As I stir and wipe and add all shapes of noodles to the warming pots, I contemplate telling Ed about Gloria's slaps. If I could ease that violation of personal space, the job may be a tick more tolerable.

"Hello, Gary. And what can I serve up for you today?"

I turn from the stock pots to face the service window. There are three men waiting behind this Gary. I step aside and watch as Gloria fills the orders and takes the men's cash. Gary and the two behind him tell Gloria to keep the change. She winks at them, leans her boobs onto the service counter and hands out their gut-growing orders.

She shows me how to cash out the cost of the meal in the register and put the leftover change in an enormous Mason jar, as big as the stock pots boiling up the fettuccini, under a curtained-off shelf near the plastics. She winks and repeats this process.

"We'll have a nice haul to split today, Jody. A dandy one."

That tip jar is the largest of its kind. Taking up valuable real estate, even. All other tip jars I've seen have been tiny drinking-glass sizes or paper ice cream cups down at the frozen yogurt place. The bills had room to float to the bottom of the jar and the coins clanked against the side in a never-ending cascade. "It'll be full by end of day," Gloria says nonchalantly and puts her hands on her waist. "You tend to the next customer by yourself. I'll get started on the rigatoni."

I turn to the window, a new eagerness welling up. Maybe this will be worth it. Butt slaps and all. "May I help you?"

The man had removed his hard hat, pressing it against his chest while he looked at the menu board propped outside the truck on the concrete.

When he faces me to order, he replaces the hat on his head revealing his nametag.

It's that rat foreman Rodney that fired my Galvis.

Well, isn't this just dandy. There goes my tip.

"I EXPECT you'll do better tomorrow." Gloria doesn't even sound angry as she helps me clean up my own mess. "Rodney is our best tipper. And our best source of referrals for all the new guys coming and going on this construction project. You'll do better tomorrow."

I'd slammed his order toward him, sloshing Miss Gloria's special triple yellow Manly-n-Cheese sauce with sausage bit topping all down the front of the service opening and all down the front of Rodney. Which I know wasn't fair, because he doesn't know who I am or why I'm so honked off. I should've told him. I really should've.

I guess Gloria thought it was a mistake. Or that I was nervous with my first solo customer.

But Rodney had it coming. Even if he didn't quite match Gal's description of a piranha with yellow teeth and red eyes. Rodney had kind blue eyes and a nice smile, but at any rate, he'd fired my bae.

So I spilled his cheese.

Even Rodney didn't seem angered by the slight. Which irritates me, now that I think about it. Shouldn't someone as bigoted as Rodney own buttons that were easy to push?

We finish wiping down the truck and Gloria wrangles the Mason jar to the floor from under the curtained counter. She tells me to dry the pots as she counts the tips.

I do what I'm told, resisting the urge to look over my shoulder at the old woman to make sure I'm not being gypped out of my fair share.

Ha. Like I earned anything today. I know good and well that I was more trouble than I was a help. I didn't deserve any of that money.

Then I think about the butt slaps and think maybe I deserve every penny of it. I can't decide.

I give the counter one final wipe, and as I turn, Gloria stuffs a wad of cash into my hand. More bills than I've ever held at once. My other jobs—temporary as they were—paid electronically via direct deposit. Before this, I'd had birthday cash from Aunt Pam, but that was always a single ten or twenty-dollar bill.

Usually a ten.

I stuff the bills into my purse, and we exit the truck out the back end of the thing. I try not to get too excited about counting the wad later and showing it to Galvis. Telling him all about the Manly cheese all over Rodney.

I take the apron off over my head and shake my hair loose. "Don't forget to wash that tonight. Crisp and clean for the morning. You have to *earn* your stains." Gloria laughed at her bad joke then gave me a final butt smack with one hand as she pulled the support beam for the serving awning closed with the other and locked the window.

She hands me a cardstock half-sheet and smiles. "This is your first day evaluation. Please drop it by the office before you come here tomorrow. Mr. Ed will be expecting it."

I take the card from her. There were spots for my name, date, hours worked. And a numbered scale—one to ten—for things like cleanliness, attitude, ability and so on.

She'd given me tens across the board with one comment in the notes section written in scrolly, happy cursive: *I know Jody will be excellent tomorrow.*

"You do know what a screw-up I am, right? I mean, tens? Really?"

"Don't be such a pasta mix, girl. Find the sunshine."

"You mean pessimist. I'm a pessimist."

"Whatever you say, sweetheart. See you tomorrow." And the great Miss Gloria waddles off toward the parking lot, twirling her dirty apron over her head.

I TURN in my card to Mr. Ed early the next morning. I'm not paid for this side-trip. I try not to think about what it costs me in gas to drive from Aunt Pam's to the office and then to the food truck's position.

He takes the card from me without reading it and piles it on a dozen or so other ones on the messy desk. I'm a little disappointed. I wanted him to see the tens. And the comment. "So how was your first day? How'd you like Miss Gloria?"

"Well, the work is okay. But I do need to let you know something." I hesitate. Turning her in after she'd given me tens and never mentioned the Rodney thing, but the butt thing is unnecessary. I explain this to Ed.

He laughs. "I know, right? She gives the best booty taps."

My jaw drops. I don't even try to stop it from falling to my chest. He sees my reaction. "Look, if you were a guy, I'd be concerned. But you're not a guy, and she's harmless."

"Really?"

"Really. You know she likes you if she's slapping your bum."

"She doesn't even know me."

"Sure she does. Gloria *knows* everyone." He belly-laughs, and I step to the side in case one of his buttons comes undone.

"Isn't that considered workplace harassment or something?"

"Let me ask you this. How are those tips?"

I bring my jaw back into submission. "Fine."

"Tips are fine. How are the customers?"

"Fine." Aside from Rodney, but even he was fine. Even after what I did.

"Customers are fine. Other than the love taps, how's Gloria?"

I sigh. "Full of dandy sunshine."

"Sun-shiny as ever. That's what I thought. Give and take, Miss Jody. Give and take." He stands from his rickety chair; it nearly topples over behind him. More papers drip off the side of his desk onto the floor where the others remain from yesterday. "If that'll be all, I'm sure Gloria is opening the truck up right about now. Time to mix the pasta." He takes a step from behind the desk.

I hustle out the door sideways on the off chance that Mr. Ed Farley wanted to slap my cheeks as well.

Traffic is light, and for that I'm thankful. I spend the drive to the work site remembering the look on Gal's face when I showed him my tips. "And that's not even all. You'll get your minimum hourly, too?"

"Yup."

"Well, bae, I may not ever have to work again." He'd propped his feet up on my dashboard. We'd spent the evening at the overlook. I wasn't sure about his unemployment. We'd make our goal faster if we were both working, but he didn't see it that way. When I brought it up again, he said I was just like Rodney. Always wanting more.

Maybe he was right. It was my turn to do some heavy lifting. He promised me the rest of the moon last night. Once we get to our new digs. Away from this awfulness. Away from the rumors and stigma.

He promised.

He's the only one I don't doubt. The only one who understands how god-awful bored I am with all things Aunt Pam and "make something of yourself" speeches.

And he said he might be by today with some of the tip money. To try out some of that Manly cheese I'd doused Rodney with. I smile. It gives me something to look forward to.

As I pull into my parking spot, I see Gloria's already propped open the service window. I reach for my apron, freshly laundered as requested.

I stretch out of my car and pull the apron on. Pull my hair back. And ready my butt cheeks for another day at the pasta office.

TRUE TO HIS word Galvis shows up at noon. Cash in hand. I beam, but Gloria has taken her break and is outside "airing out the ladies." I'm terrified to know exactly what that means, so I dare not go get her.

"How can I help you, fine sir?" I lean out toward the opening. He puts his dark arms across the service ledge.

"Manly-n-Cheese. Complete with sausage bit topping, my lady."

My heart flutters. I turn to assemble the ingredients into the Styrofoam bowl, add extra sausage and stick a fork in it. He slides me the exact amount. "What, no tip?"

"Man, girl. You don't wanna share no tip I give with that horse of a woman, do you?"

"Shhh. She'll hear." A construction worker comes up behind Gal. He steps to the side and I take his order. Exact amount for food goes into the cash drawer. His three-dollar tip goes into the jar.

When the man leaves, Gal whispers, "Just pull that out, and I'll save it back for us. She shouldn't get tips she's not working for."

"Galvis Sage?" It's Rodney. Looking very unhappy. "*Galvis?*"

"What's it to you? Free country, right?" Galvis snaps at him, but he takes a step back at the same time, his foam tray quivering in his hand.

"You know you're not supposed to be here."

"I can be where I want when I want. Paying customer, see?" He holds up his macaroni in Rodney's face.

"What's the commotion about now, Miss Jody?" Gloria steps into the truck adjusting her apron and righting her stray hairs back under the sweat band.

I can only shrug.

"Yo, who you callin', dude? I'll leave. I'll leave."

Rodney, who'd pulled out his cell and was scrolling through contacts puts the phone back in his pocket. "Leave now and don't come back."

Galvis throws his food, mostly uneaten, onto Rodney's shoes and stomps off without even looking at me.

"My, my, Rodney. You sure are a Manly-cheese magnet these days." She grabs a dirty towel from the bucket and goes to meet him. "Well, Jody. Don't just stand there. Get this hard-working man whatever he fancies and do it right quick. On the truck, Mr. Rodney."

"I'm sorry about that Miss Gloria. Just, he's got a restraining order to not be here. Before you came, he'd been late multiple times and was in safety code violations. He wouldn't come in for retraining and he'd done deliberate damage to some of the equipment. Cost us a couple thousand dollars in repairs to our machinery."

Gloria hands Rodney the towel to wipe his shoes and pant legs. She takes the lid from the trash can and scoops the fallen macaroni off to the side so no one would step in it. And I stand frozen after the commotion.

More so frozen from Rodney's news. Gal had painted his firing in a totally different picture.

"Restraining order?"

"Yes, ma'am. Endangered everyone's safety by messing with the machines. We just hope we found all he did in retaliation for getting fired. Some people think the world owes them."

"Jody. Get the man's food." Gloria is back in the truck now.

I scoop out the same order I'd made Galvis, added extra sausage even, and scooted it across the opening to Rodney. He thanks me. Takes a bite and smiles. He pulls out three bills from his pocket. I try to protest, but he shakes his head. "Miss, if you see him again, let me know. He's not to be here. He knows it. Got his papers served and everything. Court date all set. He's bad news, that one."

Gal promised me the moon. All while lying to my face.

I feel like I've been punched in the gut.

Then I feel Gloria slap my butt. "Girl. Sometimes even the smartest people make the dumbest decisions. I know you'll choose better the next time around."

The tears escape my eyes. "I hate myself. I hate my life."

I hate myself even more when I feel Gloria's massive arms pull me head-first into her massive boobs, my cheek pressed hard against her reading glasses. "Now, gather yourself, my little pasta mix. We've got a line forming."

I sniff and dry my face on my apron before turning to face the crowd. "It's pessimist. I'm a pessimist. And there is no sunshine in this, so don't even go there."

Gloria smiles at me. Gives me one more slap. "Give and take, girl. Give and take."

GLORIA'S SUNSHINE and my rainclouds make for some interesting conversation in between boiling rigatoni, browning sausage, and stirring marinara. Somchow this woman I don't really care for has dug out my flawed logic in choosing Galvis. Logic that I knew down deep was flawed, but didn't care because he was my ticket away, or so I thought.

She also pulled out plans for my future, which I didn't know I had. How much I really did admire and love Aunt Pam, which I also knew but didn't take the time to examine.

Miss Gloria the optimist is god-awful annoying. And she can't say "pessimist" to save her life. It always comes out "pasta mix."

But she shares her tips. Right down the middle. The last four weeks, I've made enough money to take me and Galvis further than we'd ever imagined. But Galvis is no more. I blocked his sorry rump weeks ago—faster than Gloria could slap mine.

Rodney has been a source of ever-present macaroni orders. And three three-dollar tips a day. Four-fifty a day extra. Just for slopping out carbs to the foreman.

And every time Rodney's around, Gloria elbows me in my gut and winks. "See the sunshine?" and "Isn't he a dandy?" Over and over again.

I've been three more times to see Mr. Ed with those half-cards. Always filled with tens. Always a scrolly cursive compliment. Always thrown into a stack and never read.

And I still dodge his too-tight shirt buttons.

Today I arrive to find Rodney organizing a crew on the gigantic crane that arrived yesterday along with massive steel beams. They tell me, and I hear the men talk, that their crew is almost done with their part of the building. The crane is the last bit of work. After that, Gloria and I will relocate.

I'll miss the construction site. But she misses her loyals downtown, so downtown we shall go. She'll bring the butt-slapping sunshine. I'll bring the snark and clouds.

Gloria is opening the truck, as always, earlier than me and sunnier. I hear Rodney barking orders to his crew. I see the crane's arm swing over to the pile of beams. I go into the food truck.

It's louder today.

"Maybe we should move the truck. Just in case." I speak up over the crane's engine and metal-on-metal screeching.

"Give and take, miss Jody. We're fine right here. Right close to the action and all the hungry men." She goes about her morning prep. Filling pots with water. Shaking spices and seasonings into melting cheese and sizzling sausages. The humidity rises in the food truck's interior, steaming up the metallic walls and wafting curls of smoke out of the service opening. I'm in my routine of wiping, stirring, cleaning when I hear it.

Or maybe I feel it first. I can't decide.

The metal-on-metal turns to metal-on-shrieks and rumbles. A quake. A tremor really. Nothing new. But the crane doesn't know that.

"Miss Gloria let's move now."

But my warning is too late. The floor shakes under my feet. I'm not sure if from the earth moving or the crane. The crane's arm— or maybe the steel beam it was trying to hoist moments ago—falls. The metal roof of the food truck is no match for the weight of whatever and the shaking doesn't stop. I'm two feet from the back of the door. Gloria's not so fast.

The top of the truck buckles further, breaking apart the welding and seams. The sturdy stock pots dump their boiling contents all over the floor. Gloria slips to her knees, cries out from the burns and the shrinking space. She holds her hands above her head, but she doesn't try to stand.

Shouts echo off the metal. Above the din outside. Rodney. Yells for me to get out.

Tells me to leave her.

But I can't.

He tells me he's cutting the power and the gas and the…I stop listening and join Gloria on my knees on the floor of the truck. The ceiling comes lower and lower. More and more daylight seeps through. The lights in the truck go off. The flames from the burners, now tipping toward us die out.

Rodney must've cut the lines.

She's pinned to her stomach now, crying. Sobbing. In the steamy bath of rigatoni and marinara. All over the floor. All over her. She's pinned.

I feel the heat of the lunch remnants rise onto my knees and thighs.

The truck struggles, making a final stand against the fallen iron above. The ceiling gives one last jerk toward the floor, and now I'm on my stomach. But she's taking the brunt of it. I see red. I think it's marinara, but the color's off.

She's bleeding.

I grab behind me for a stock pot. The one that's heavy as sin and big enough for three small dogs. I'd seen it topple seconds ago. I feel it's familiar handle. The metal is still warm.

I drag it over my body and put it near her chest.

Just in time. The pot holds enough of the ceiling/beam combo away from her rib cage. If those boobs weren't so massive we'd have more room to work.

"Hurry up. Help," I scream to Rodney. Or whoever's listening. "Hang on Gloria. I'm staying with you."

"Go, Jody. Get out."

"Nope. Give and take. Give and take, old woman."

I try to shift and see if I can dislodge her from the ceiling, but the weight of the beam and whatever she's caught on from the knees down resists, and she cries out afresh. "Okay. Okay. It'll be okay. Tomorrow, when we're all patched up, we'll go down to Mr. Ed's and order us a new pasta truck."

She lets out a half-laugh, half-cry. "Look at you. Little Miss Sunshine."

"No, Gloria, I'm a pasta mix, remember?"

"Whatever you say, girl. Whatever you…"

She fades out.

"No, Gloria. No. Don't you dare." I run my hands through her salt-and-pepper hair. Her sweatband lies in a soupy mess three feet away. Her reading glasses lay in pieces, some shards near her. I imagine the other parts are under her. I pat her cheeks. "Wake up, Gloria."

I feel water. Cold water. Someone shouts again. I hear sirens. Maybe I heard sirens before the water. I can't decide. The truck shakes again and I pray the pot holds.

Then I feel hands around my ankles. Pulling "No. I'm staying with her." I fight against my rescuer.

"We have to move you to get to her. Let us work." Rodney.

Pulling. Ceiling giving just ever so slightly again. Stock pot holding steady.

Another rumble.

Then all goes black.

~

I WAKE up under seriously intense lights. Hands all over me. In my personal space. And I fight back.

Rodney, kind blue eyes and a smile equally kind, stands over me. "Easy. You're in the ER. Your aunt is on her way. You're okay. You hit your head—or rather, we may have hit your head pulling you out. Sorry for that."

"Gloria?"

"Upstairs. Stable. Thanks to you. Quick thinking with that stock pot."

I sit up, pulling on wires and buzzers. He tries to stop me, but I push his hands away. "You don't like to cooperate, do you?"

"Nope." I continue to unhook IV lines and blood pressure cuff. A couple of nurses try to stop me, but I demand to see Gloria. Then I compromise with them. Give and take. They can do what they want to me after I see Gloria, pretty please.

They give.

Rodney goes with me upstairs.

Mr. Ed Farley is at her bedside. She's sitting up. Head bandaged. Legs wrapped. Arm in a sling. All smiles and sunshine.

When Ed moves aside, I see the stock pot sitting on the bedside table, filled with fresh-cut flowers. I point and laugh.

"Miss Jody, this pot will be our new tip jar. My Mason bit the dust and part of it lodged in my ankle." She wiggled her feet, and Mr. Ed put his hand on her knee gently to stop her.

He leans down and kisses her on the forehead. She slaps him on the butt.

My jaw drops.

"Oh, don't look so surprised, Miss Jody. He is my husband, after all."

Well that explains a thing or two.

Ed reaches into a black trash bag on the other side of the bed and pulls out my purse, soaking wet, and my apron. It's covered in reds and yellows and blacks and who knows what else.

"You'll have to wash that up tonight. Be ready bright and early in the morning."

"You're kidding me. That apron is ruined. I'll need a new one. And you can't possibly think that tomorrow—"

The Farleys laugh at me. I shake my head. It's like having the world's corniest grandparents. The ones that push your buttons because you've got so many buttons to push and you can't do anything about it because, well, because they're family.

And you love them.

Gloria motions for me to come close. She slaps my butt then takes my throbbing temples in her hands and pulls me into her massive boobs. The most massive, kindest hug I've ever had. "When we get a new truck, you'll wear that apron proudly. Because you certainly earned those stains, my favorite little pasta mix."

The Smiley Face Fence on Brookdale Drive

When the city comes after Tabby's childhood—and the childhood of dozens of foster kids just like her—it's time to take a stand.

*T*abby brushed her daughter's unruly curls into a pony-tail and scooted her out the door. The dew glistened on the front lawn. She buckled the three-year-old into the booster. Tabby had to run the wipers and roll down the front windows to clear them before she could leave the drive.

She had an eight o'clock appointment with the mortuary. The visitation and funeral services last week went well, and Tabby was listed in the will as Miss Agnes Littleton's executor. She was also listed as the one who should receive Agnes's ashes to do with as she saw fit.

Tabby had no idea what to do with them. Her husband said it would be creepy to leave them in the house, even though neither was superstitious or overly concerned with such matters.

She pulled into the lot, retrieved her daughter and went inside. Kelly squirmed and kicked to break free, but it wasn't the time or the place. Tabby whispered a harsh correction into Kelly's ear, and the little girl settled and allowed her mother to tote her to the mortician's office.

"Hello, Mrs. Sutton. Thank you for making it here so early. We have a viewing this afternoon for a serviceman with complicated wishes." The lady seemed frazzled, dropping papers and shifting files across the desk.

She unlocked the bottom filing cabinet drawer and pulled out a black box the size of the shoe box that Kelly's last sneakers had come in. One woman's existence reduced to such a small piece of real estate.

Tabby signed the paperwork. "What can I do with them? Do you have any suggestions?"

The lady shuffled more papers, looking under this pile and that, and finally produced a sheet. "Here are some guidelines and prices if you'd want to use the cemetery. They can open a spot near a family member's headstone for a hundred fifty. But," she leaned in close and whispered, "if you ask me, you can just talk a nice walk and scatter them. No harm done in my opinion. No need to file for permission or pay all that extra."

Tabby folded the paper and slid it into her jeans. She thanked the lady, though she'd not been much help, and gathered the box and Kelly.

"Oh, Mrs. Sutton, they're setting up in the main room now. Would you mind leaving out the side door?"

"Sure." Tabby walked through the side, where Agnes had lain in a rented casket for the viewing in a smaller, more secluded room. Tabby remembered the small trickle of people who'd paid their respects to the old lady. She'd spent most of her last two years in a nursing home. Tabby had tried to visit as much as she could, but with Kelly it was difficult. She didn't know how Agnes got anything done in her years with the kids. Many of those kids came to the viewing. Many couldn't make it. And Agnes, at eighty-six years old, had outlived some of her children.

Tabby buried her face in Kelly's hair, breathed in the strawberry shampoo to erase the swell of emotion, and left the building.

McDonald's drive-thru was just what Tabby needed to distract Kelly for a moment so she could think. Tom really didn't want the ashes in the house, and neither did Tabby. Agnes wouldn't want to rest in a box in some closet or put on display in a fancy urn. She'd want to be set free in some meaningful place.

She pulled into the park and sat Kelly on the picnic bench with the Happy Meal toy she'd paid extra for because they weren't serving lunch yet.

Agnes had liked the park. Tabby could simply empty the box of the contents along the shady row of oaks where the landscapers had recently planted red and pink impatiens. In a few weeks, the flowers would propagate, cover Miss Agnes, and everyone would be happy.

But it felt empty, too easy. Tabby needed more time to think.

She needed inspiration.

She called Tom's mom and asked if she was free to watch Kelly for a while. "Absolutely," came the answer. Tabby would pay for it later as her mother-in-law rarely enforced nap time and treated Kelly to all manner of sugary delights and wild rumpus.

"Want to go see Granny?"

Kelly's blue eyes lit up and she squealed and ran for the van.

Tabby caught her half-way there, hanging her upside down in playful glee. "Will you be good for Granny?"

Giggles and nods from the topsy-turvy girl, her ponytail brushing the ground.

"Are you sure?"

"Yessss, Mommy!"

Tabby turned her right side up and fastened her into the seat once more. After dropping her off with her grandmother and "kissies" goodbye, Tabby headed for her girlhood home for the first time in ten years.

BROOKDALE DRIVE WAS on the other side of the city. Tabby had returned only once since graduating high school—when Agnes was first diagnosed with cancer about a decade ago. The sweet lady enjoyed remission for a while, but the chemotherapy damaged her liver so badly that she became too weak to live on her own. Agnes had spent the rest of her days in a nursing home on the east side, near Tabby.

She pulled onto the road, and the two-story childhood home called attention to itself, distracting the view from the well-kept homes all along Brookdale. Tabby would have liked to think it was because the house had sat empty for so long, but that wasn't the case. The home had always stood out as odd.

Agnes Littleton's home was the oldest in the neighborhood by far. Other owners had sold or renovated their homes decades ago, but not Agnes. She'd put her heart and soul into her kids, not the house. It had served one purpose: to give haven to as many as possible.

Once Agnes fell ill, she'd made Tabby promise not to get rid of it until she was "good and dead." Tabby had received notices from the city council that it should be leveled, or at least handed over to a developer or flipped. The empty dwelling was drawing all manner of vandalism and the occasional squatter. She'd given them permission to board up the windows and doors, but informed them that

Agnes, still in her right mind, had no mind to sell or demolish the property.

The neighbors' complaints escalated so that as soon as the preacher said "Amen" after the funeral, Tabby and Tom had received notice from dutiful councilwoman Vickie Snyder, conveniently in attendance that day, that if they'd sign the papers, which were conveniently in her vehicle, demolition could begin as soon as possible and the whole matter would be out of Tabby's hair. Of course, she was doing the Suttons a favor by expediting the process.

That had been a week ago.

Today, on Brookdale Drive under a cloudless summer sky, Tabby saw the two-story, wood-sided house on the large corner lot for what it was: her first real home. She pulled along the curb by the fence and put the van in park. She looked at the little black box in the seat next to her and sobbed.

She'd cried when she'd heard the news of Agnes's passing, of course. She'd shed tears at the viewing and again at the funeral. But real grief had evaded her until the moment the wooden privacy fence stretching the length of the property came into full view.

Agnes had taken Tabby into her home when Tabby was ten years old and her parents had died in a car accident. There were no relatives, or at least no one that had wanted her, and Agnes's foster home had had an empty bedroom.

Or that's what Agnes had told Child Protective Services.

Agnes had filed for foster parent status when she was forty-five, after her husband passed away. The couple never had children, which Agnes had desperately longed for. She took in as many as would fit in the five-bedroom home. Many times, she'd give up her own bedroom to allow siblings to stay together. She'd sleep on the couch and never complain about it.

CPS had placed Tabby in the fifth bedroom.

And Agnes had ended up on the couch.

She'd ran the home like a miniature army boot camp, but with all the love of a grandmother. Every kid, after a day or two, knew the routine, the schedule and their responsibilities. They only stepped out of line once or twice. Agnes had a way about her that no one could quite describe. The look of disappointment in her pale blue eyes was enough for even the hard-nosed gang teen to bow their head in submission and comply with her requests.

Tabby dried the tears and stepped out of the van. She walked along Brookdale toward 5th Street and admired the fence. Eight feet high and made of simple plank wood, it surrounded the entire property. Neighbors on the Brookdale side claimed it drove their property values down. Those on the 5th Street side demanded the fence be painted. Agnes had explained to the city council that her children needed to be kept safe, and that it would be worse for the neighbors if the balls, bikes and hula hoops were in eye-shot. It was the fence or the mess.

Agnes had won out with the stipulation that she paint the fence.

She signed the paperwork stating, "The fence shall be painted yearly."

"I'll do them one better. We'll paint it every few months."

Tabby had been with Agnes about two months when the paint issue arose. She remembered coming to Agnes's from school that day. Agnes had gallons of paint, all in different shades—skin tones, pastels, bolds and brights. She had five gallons of black. She whistled for the children, eight of them that day. Seven of them lined up in front of her, and she carried three-year-old Billy on her hip.

"Today, we're gonna paint this fence." She handed each child a paintbrush, allowed them to pick their favorite color and directed them to the outside of the fence. She spread the kids along the sidewalk, some along Brookdale, some along 5th Street. She handed Billy to Fredrico, one of the teenage boys. "This is how it's gonna work."

She spread her arms out as far as she could get them and hugged against the fence, face pressed sideways against the wooden planks. "Have a friend mark where your fingertips end. Then we'll paint a huge circle that wide in some happy color. When that color dries, we'll paint on black eyes and a smiley face mouth."

She took Billy and stood his back against the fence and spread his arms out "like an airplane." Tabby remembered thinking the woman had lost it. All these years of caring for the kids, and she'd just snapped. She set three choices in front of the little boy. He picked sky blue.

She opened the can, dipped in a brush and put a mark at the ends of his fingertips, and then a dot of blue on his nose, which made everyone giggle. She moved him out of the way and showed them how to make two arcs to form a big circle. "No need for perfection. Ain't none of us perfect anyway."

The other seven kids got to work, helping each other mark out the width of the faces. Older kids took up the top portions of the fence, letting the younger ones have the lower parts. Most of them chose wild and wonderful colors. Fredrico chose a rich tan to match his skin.

While the circles dried, she sat them down on the sidewalk, praised them for their efforts and explained that each time a new child came to the home, they'd find a place on the fence to paint their smiley face. And when and if the time came for a child to leave Agnes's foster home, they could paint a fabulous hat of their own creation as a way to say goodbye.

Tabby stopped midway on Brookdale, directly under the street lamp. After all this time, Tabby could still find her smiley face. She spread her arms over the fence and her painted face, once hot pink, now faded to pastel with gray eyes and a fading smile. Her fingertips reached beyond the edges of her face and touched the neighboring artwork.

Tabby had stayed with Agnes until she "adulted out." After graduation, she had to find her own way and make room for another child under Agnes's roof. The day before she left, after she'd packed her things, five kids, all different ages and all different from the ones who'd started the smiley face fence eight years before, lined up to watch Tabby paint the hat onto her face.

Over the years, Tabby, and many other kids, filled notebooks with different hat designs, dreaming of adoption or graduation, in anticipation of leaving Miss Agnes. Not that they wanted to leave. None of them were mistreated, but every foster kid's hope is for some sense of permanence. Tabby had settled on a black gradua-tion cap with a purple and yellow tassel. The kids all clapped and cheered. Miss Agnes hugged her so tight that day that Tabby thought her insides would burst.

She walked a few feet down to Fredrico's face. He never got to paint a hat on his artwork. Tabby reached up and traced the halo with her fingers. Sometimes, no matter how much Agnes tried, things just didn't turn out. In her magnificent stretch as a foster mother, Agnes had lost five children. Three faces on Brookdale and two faces on 5th Street wore halos. Five lives snuffed out from the ugliness of drugs, gangs or crazed birth parents.

An obnoxious alarm pulled Tabby from the past. She turned back to see a bulldozer and several other vehicles lining the street in front of the house.

A hard-hatted worker approached with a clipboard. "Are you here to sign the papers?"

"No, I don't think so."

"I thought you were Vickie Synder."

"No, I'm not."

"That's me, that's me!" Vickie came around the corner from 5th Street, high heels clacking on the pavement. "I'll sign it. Sorry I'm late." She took the clipboard and flew through the paperwork. To Tabby she said, "I didn't know you'd be here today."

"It's happening today? You're tearing it down today?"

"Yes, ma'am. If there's anything in the house you want saved, you'll need to go get it now."

Tabby stared at the fence. Dozens of faces smiled back at her, in every color imaginable. Dozens more down on 5th.

"I want the fence," she whispered.

"What's that?" asked Vickie.

"The fence. I don't want the fence damaged."

"Well, ma'am, the fence can't stay. We have to take it down to reach the house." The construction worker pushed hard along the fence, testing for weaknesses.

"I don't care what you do with the house. But I want the fence left intact."

"That's not possible, Mrs. Sutton." Vickie stood with a hand on her hip.

"You said I could save what I wanted. I want the fence." Tabby was panicking. A worker fired up the bulldozer and repositioned it to take down the first section. Tabby moved to block it.

"Mrs. Sutton, you must move. You can't impede this work!"

"Watch me." Never in her life had Tabby felt so defiant. She sat down in front of the fence, between it and the dozer. She pulled out her phone and took a photo of the scene, of councilwoman Vickie and the construction crew, who were now on their phones, no doubt to the police.

As fast as she could, she uploaded the photos to Facebook and tagged as many of her foster siblings as she could. Many of them still lived in the area. Some of them, like Tabby, had managed to find permanence with a family of their own.

"Mrs. Sutton, you must move. You're hindering the work scheduled for today."

"Just give me a little bit of time." Tabby stood and faced Vickie. Neighbors gathered on their lawns, watching the show.

Within ten minutes, two cop cars and another three council people arrived on Brookdale Drive. Tabby explained the situation, as slowly as she could to buy more time, and after another ten minutes, five of the foster siblings showed up, two with spouses. They spread themselves across Brookdale and down the 5th Street side.

After another twenty minutes, both sides doubled—four cops and seven council people versus over a dozen of Miss Agnes's children, many now with children of their own. The fosters, almost by instinct, stood as near their own smiley faces as they could, unmoving.

The crowd gathered from the neighborhood and someone called the local news station. Tabby spotted Tom in the crowd, holding their daughter, whom she'd forgotten to pick up from her mother-in-law's in all the commotion. She tried to read his face, fearful that he'd be angry with her. But before she could see him clearly, he lifted a fist in the air and shouted, "Save That Fence! Save That Fence!"

Tabby bawled. The crowd, even some of the opinionated neighbors, got swept up in the chant. The Channel Seven News camera swept the scene, showing the contrast of the honked off officials gathered at the corner in their business suits versus the lively fist-pumpers. The cops were forced to redirect traffic around the mess.

Along the fence, Miss Agnes's children stood strong, joining hands while the dozens of colorful faces smiled on.

Then someone called the mayor.

AFTER TWO WEEKS of fighting and planning, Tabby Sutton and a dozen of her siblings won the right to move the fence. Gently.

They declared a work day, and the families showed up on Brookdale Drive to disassemble the fence, laying the planked sections on rented and borrowed flatbed trailers. The construction crew oversaw the project, and once the fence was down and the crowd had moved to a safe distance, many of them stayed to watch the initial demolition of the home in which they had been so well cared for.

Tabby, Tom, Kelly and Miss Agnes's black box joined in the caravan from Brookdale to the public park near Tabby's neighborhood. The same one she'd thought about scattering Agnes in weeks ago.

After a morning of work, the gang reconstructed the fence along the perimeter of the park. The news crew did follow-up interviews and took sweeping shots of the massive project. Gallons of paint donated by the local hardware store in every color imaginable came out, along with paintbrushes and smocks for the little ones. Each foster worked over their smiley face, keeping the original dimensions and colors as true as possible to the first day it was painted. For those that weren't able to make it, someone's spouse or child brightened up their smiley face for them.

Tabby took special care with Fredrico's smiley face and the halo Miss Agnes had painted herself years ago.

They replanted the impatiens along the base of the fence, then Tom stood on a picnic tabletop and called order to the group.

Tabby took the black box from the funeral home and opened the pouch inside.

"Rest in peace, Miss Agnes Littleton." Tabby laid her to rest along the base of the fence, forever smiled over by her children.

The crowd cheered and cried. Tabby joined her forever family for a huge embrace until Kelly wiggled away and pointed at the fence.

"Look at all the happy, Mommy!"

Tabby tipped her little girl upside down and swung her around. "Kelly Agnes Sutton! I love you."

Leftovers

Scripture's momma always told him he'd do great things. And do great things he did… Laugh. Cry. Or, maybe don't laugh quite yet, as Scripture Jennings lets you peek into his world for an afternoon or two…
First printed in Issue 8 of Pulphouse Fiction Magazine and edited by Dean Wesley Smith, "Leftovers" features one of B.A. Paul's most memorable characters.

*O*nce in a while, the good people of Hickory Hills asked Scripture Jennings for his help.

And Scripture was always happy to help.

Scripture walked down Main Street to the tiny stone funeral parlor. Gwen had called him the night before with a job. It had been a while since anyone had called him with work, but the little town of Hickory Hills didn't have many jobs for someone like Scripture.

Colorful pastel flags indicating the weekend of the Rainbow Run decked the rooftops up and down Main. Scripture paused for a moment, put his hands deep into his overall pockets, and gazed at the dancing flags. The residents would line the streets and throw colored powder all over each other and high into the air as they ran, skipped, and walked all over downtown Hickory.

Scripture's momma hadn't had the means to keep him in school. Scripture dropped out to help take care of his momma after she fell sick with the cancer. Since she died, he lived meagerly in their family home at the far edge of town and depended on a small trust she'd set up for him for his adulthood.

His momma did teach him how to be kind and caring and to work hard. "You're gonna do great things, Scripture Jennings, when you don't have to look after this old bag of bones any more. You're gonna do great things."

And Scripture had done things he was proud of, but he didn't think they counted as

great things.

Like when old farmer Ted had trouble with coyotes attacking his cows out by the edge of town. Ted called Scripture to help with the fences. And Scripture took down every one of those fences while Ted tended to his day job so those cows could find a safe place to hide in the woods on the other side of Interstate 265. The traffic on the highway helped out, too, by waiting patiently for six hours while the cows crossed the road. He'd done a good thing for Mr. Ted.

And then there was the time that Scripture helped Councilwoman Cynthia when the ivy vines overgrew the City Hall building. Scripture went right to work, clipping and cutting that ivy away from the walls so those good lawmakers could see out of their windows and the townspeople could see the pretty red brickwork. That nasty ivy even climbed the poles on the corner of the street. Scripture's momma would be proud that he did his best and even cleared those poles, clipping and cutting some more.

The store owners on that side of Main jumped right in and helped, too, since some of them didn't have any power to their buildings and had nothing better to do. Even the electric company came out to lend a hand.

He felt proud of his work that day, too. But he didn't think it was great.

He smiled up at the flags because tonight he got to mix up all the colored powder for the race. It was his most favorite job for over ten years now. And, during the race, he would stand on top of the bakery's roof to watch the festivities. He never accepted pay for preparing the colored packets. He only asked that he could watch from above and cheer on the runners.

But this morning, he hoped to be paid because he was running low on funds since he'd spent his last week's allowance on feed and toys for the pet shelter. He planned to do the best he could for Miss Gwen.

He arrived at the parlor where Gwen smiled at him from the front steps. Scripture was a little nervous about coming here today, because his momma was here just a year ago and he didn't much like the day that he watched over her in the casket; he still wished his momma hadn't had to go.

Since Scripture's momma didn't have funds left for a proper burial after setting up his trust, Scripture had agreed to cremate her. Gwen graciously performed that service for Scripture without charge since the tiny parlor operated the only crematorium for miles around. He'd tucked his momma's ashes away in a little white box in the kitchen cabinet. She loved the kitchen, and Scripture watched over her each morning to be sure she was safe and sound.

"Hey, Scrip. Are you ready to get to work? I have a lot to do to get ready for the race, so I'm so glad you could be here today." Gwen gave Scripture a big hug and escorted him through the oak door. Gwen had called him "Scrip" ever since she was a little girl. If he'd a little sister, he'd want her to be just like Gwen.

"Yes, Miss Gwen. Happy to do whatever." He shoved his hands back in his overalls and focused on the warped wooden floor. Thinking about his momma made him tear up, and he hoped Gwen didn't notice.

"I'd like to clean out the attic today, and I thought you'd be perfect for the job." She nodded toward a door marked *Do Not Enter.* "Nothing up there needs to be saved. Everything will be donated or disposed of. All you have to do is bring everything downstairs to the back dock, and George will sort it all out. Do you understand?"

Scripture nodded. "Yes, Miss Gwen. Everything goes to the back dock." Scripture learned over the years that people liked him to repeat directions back. He figured it helped them out somehow. Even his momma asked him to repeat things.

"On the dock, there are bins for the smaller items. If anything is too heavy for you, let me know and I'll have George come help. Okay?" Gwen unlocked the attic door and opened it for him. She flipped the light switch and Scripture peered up the narrow staircase.

"Okay. I'll put items in the bins and then ask George if somethin's too heavy." Scripture grinned big. "But, Miss Gwen, you know I'm a pretty strong guy."

Gwen patted him on the shoulder. "Yes, you sure are. Your momma sure grew you up strong. I'll be down at City Hall if you need anything."

He beamed and started up the steps. "I'll do a good job for you, Miss Gwen."

"I know you will."

Scripture reached the landing of the attic. Three bare bulbs hung from the ceiling, highlighting the dust he'd stirred up with his feet. Momma always told him to pick up his feet, but he still shuffled them from time to time.

The attic was full of boxes overflowing with bits and pieces of décor, some of it matching what was downstairs. Other boxes held tubing and glass vials and vases and stationery with pens that had

"Hickory Hills Funeral Parlor" printed on the barrels. He tried one of the ink pens on his hand, but the ink didn't flow. A roll of green floral carpet leaned against a bookcase full of thick, heavy books. He could read some of the titles well enough, but they didn't look interesting at all.

He started to sweat from the stuffy quarters, and the dust collected in the droplets on his forehead. He didn't think he saw anything that he would need George's help with, which was good. He didn't like splitting his wage with someone.

He made trips one after the other down the narrow steps. One time, he lost his footing and dropped a box full of artificial poinsettias. It didn't take him long to clean it up, and he was back to work quickly. He would pause on the small dock outside after each trip to breathe the fresh air and rid his nostrils of the stale dust of the attic.

On the way back up the steps the next time, he figured he had two more trips: one for the carpet, because the roll was as big as him, and one for the now-empty bookcase. He slid the roll onto his shoulder just how his momma used to carry bags of potatoes from Ted's garden over her shoulders, and delivered it to the dock. He wiped his dusty sweat and headed up again.

He slid the bookcase away from the wall and tipped it onto its side for the final journey down the stairs. But there, behind the bookcase, rows of shelving hung between the open studs. Five rows of boxes lined the narrow shelving. Boxes like his momma rested in now at home in the kitchen cabinet.

Scripture set the bookcase down and stared at the boxes. Thick dust covered each, and none were as white as the one his momma was in. Some were yellow and some were brown, but all were the same size.

He pulled one off the middle shelf and took it to the center of the room under the light. He blew across the top of the box, revealing a typed label. He rubbed his thumb over the label to remove the last layer of dust.

The Cremated Remains of one Samuel Preston, November 1986.

He gently opened the lid and inside was a small, thick plastic bag, weighing just a couple of pounds. That was all that was left of his momma, too. He closed the lid and noticed on the side of the box was a sticker with a single handwritten word.

Unclaimed.

He placed Mr. Preston on the tipped-over bookcase and chose the first box from the very top shelf. This yellowed box seemed to have more dust than the others. He blew the dust off and wiped the top of it on the butt of his overalls.

The Cremated Remains of one Sarah Anne Knight, August 1967.

He turned the box to its side.

Unclaimed.

Scripture's heart began to ache and he could smell his sweat now, rolling from every pore in his face. His hands shook just like the day he'd carried his momma home from this very place.

He chose another box.

The Cremated Remains of one Marie Bennington, June 1979.

Unclaimed.

Scripture stopped choosing boxes and, instead, twisted them around on the shelf to see their sides.

Unclaimed.

Unclaimed.

Unclaimed.

Tears flowed freely, mingled with dust and sweat.

Surely Gwen didn't know these were here. She would never treat people like this. She would have found a home for them, Scripture was positive of that. He sat down next to Mr. Preston on the bookcase's side and wiped his sweat. Here he was, a great big grown man crying alone in an attic. What would his momma think?

Donated or destroyed. That's what Gwen had said.

He just couldn't. He just couldn't.

He put Mr. Preston back on the shelf with the others and carried the bookcase down to the dock. George had already backed up his pickup truck and was loading the dusty junk into the bed.

"Mr. George, Mr. George, hold up!" Scripture helped George load the bookcase and the cumbersome carpet roll. "Can I have one of these bins for tomorrow?"

"Anything you need from out here, Scripture. That's just fine."

Scripture nodded his thanks and grabbed a large plastic bin from the dock, stopped in the small kitchenette just inside the back door and grabbed a roll of paper towel and headed back to the attic one last time.

He approached the shelf and loaded each box into the bin, blowing dust off the tops, then wiping them on the butt, chest or legs of his overalls as he went. He counted twenty-five in all.

Twenty-five unclaimed lives.

Leftovers.

He unrolled several sheets of toweling and covered the top layer of boxes with it. He wished he had a lid, but the bin was over-flowing so it wouldn't do either way. He hefted it onto his hip and surveyed the attic. Everything was out. Just like Miss Gwen asked him to do.

He went down the stairs and turned off the lights.

Dirt and dust from several decades covered Scripture's overalls. And he smelled bad, but he had another job to do this evening.

He made his way a few blocks down Main to the bakery where the kind Mr. Mark set up the mixer and all the ingredients for the Rainbow Run.

"Hey there, Scripture! I was about to give up on you and call in extra help to make the packets. Hey, can I give you a hand with that?" Mr. Mark's white apron was covered in dirt, too. Probably chocolate, though, not attic dust, because the air here smelled of cake and cookies.

"No, sir. I've got this. Just some extra supplies for tomorrow." Scripture wasn't exactly telling the truth, and he wasn't exactly lying. Somewhere in the muddy middle.

"You look like you've been working hard today. Here. I have an apron that will fit over your dusty clothes. We wouldn't want our color packs to be brown, now would we?" Mr. Mark laughed as he pulled a large apron off the hook over the door. Scripture laughed with him and put on the apron.

"Just like last year, okay, Scripture? Everything you need is here on the counter." Mark nodded to the row of corn starch, a rainbow of powdered food dyes and hundreds of baggies.

"Just like last year, Mr. Mark." Scripture would be up all night mixing and filling.

Mark left Scripture alone in the bakery. He started the mixer up just like Mark had shown him ten years ago and measured in the white starch first.

Then in went the pink powdered dye.

And then in went Sarah Anne Knight and Miss Marie Bennington.

He found three other ladies and added them to the mix as well. He had to add in extra pink to brighten things up after the gray ashes of the women dulled the mix. He bagged up the pinks and set them aside.

It was dark outside now. He'd have to hurry his pace if he was going to get all the colors made by morning.

Whistling now, he added in more corn starch and chose the blue dye. Once those were mixing well, Mr. Preston joined in, along with four other men from the funeral parlor's bin. And he bagged up the blues.

Yellow was next. He wasn't sure how to divvy up yellow, because well, that was confusing. He added a couple of ladies and a couple of men and one name he couldn't read so he wasn't sure.

Purple was all ladies.

Green had all men.

Everyone had a purpose. And everyone would be as free as Mr. Ted's cows.

None were left over.

His white apron was a pastel rainbow with shades of gray like storm clouds. He didn't think any of the folks would mind, so long as most of each of them could be free of their boxes and the attic.

The stainless steel table that held all of the ingredients hours ago now held hundreds and hundreds of baggies of color. He took off the apron, turned off the light and headed home just as the sun was coming up. The race would start in a few hours, so he had to hurry.

Despite the lack of sleep and food, he felt better than he had since before his momma got sick. He changed into a fresh pair of overalls, stuffed a banana from the counter into his deep overall pocket, grabbed his momma from the cabinet and stuffed her box between the bib and his t-shirt.

He reached the bakery to find Gwen passing out the color baggies to the racers. "Good job on the attic, Scrip! I'm so glad you got that done. And what a good job on the packets! They look brighter every year." Scripture beamed and nodded his thanks.

He headed to the back of the bakery where he could access the stairs to the roof. The race was about to start, and he didn't want his momma to miss it.

Excited residents of Hickory Hills lined up at the starting line at City Hall (where you could see every red brick on the building because the ivy was gone now). It was George's turn to blow the whistle for the marathon this year, and he did it just fine and right on time.

Everyone cheered and lots of people started throwing their colored powder right away. Some of them waited, though, and when the mass of people neared the bakery just under Scripture, he watched as fifty or so of them sent up a swirling cloud of pink ladies and blue men and all the others.

Scripture whispered to his momma about the great thing he finally did.

And he set her free, too.

Half Staff

After Michelle's father dies in the line of duty, the ceremonial lowering of the flags to half-staff ceased—there are just too many fallen officers to bother with the ritual any longer. In her grief, or maybe in spite of it, Michelle decides to honor her father the only way she knows how.

I'd realized I'd grossly underestimated my need for gloves on the long walk to the middle tower. I'd journeyed the walkway along the suspension bridge connecting our shore with our neighbors' dozens of times with my father and sister—when she felt well enough to come. But I'd never done it in the fog. I'd never come alone. And I'd never needed to cling to the handrails with such a grip.

That'd been a couple of hours ago. Now, the walkway rests dozens of feet below me. I try not to think about it down there. Uncaring concrete and cold metal waiting to catch me should I slip.

Because I'm a chicken. My sister was right.

I cup my hands in front of my face and blow into them. I draw my knees up to my chest. Most of the rest of me, wrapped in cozy layers, is dry and warm. Well, all but my butt which soaks up the damp from the metal grate of the landing. Landing three. I'd only ever been brave enough to make it to the second landing. But not this morning. This morning I need to make it to the top of the tower, but I'm shaking so badly that I don't trust my legs.

I can swim. Dad made sure of that. But I couldn't swim if I hit metal stair casings and the roadway before landing in the river.

The bridge is still sleepy. Only the occasional car rumbles below. Those early commuters or perhaps those coming off a weary late shift. I try not to think about what's below too much—my focus needs to remain on the pole above me. The metal rivets and tie-backs on the flagpole ding and clang above me. Calling me higher.

Telling me to get off my wet, frozen butt and scale up to another landing. One at a time.

But I'm a chicken.

From my near-fetal position, breathing warmth into my palms, I strain to see across the river, but the lights from my home are shrouded in the fog. From this height, I'd thought I could spot our window. I know my sister's watching. She begged me not to come out here. To let it go.

But I couldn't.

The river sloshes against the supports of the suspension bridge below. Way below. Down past those occasional sleepy drivers. I'm grateful I can't see the murk of the water. That I can't tell how fast the river churns and flows this morning. I can't tell how high the swell is after the rains they had up north. I'm not sure if that rain has made it to my bridge. Above me, in between the flag pole's impatient dinging, I hear the occasional plane. Red-Eyes readying for landing. Business class fliers waiting for the all clear from the cockpit to lower their tray tables and fire up their laptops. But I can't see the planes' white or red lights. The fog's too thick.

Three landings. Three more to go. I try not to think about the height.

The grate digs into my thighs. I run a hand over it. The landing feels as if a madman shot bullets from underneath, piercing the thick metal upward in jagged alligator mouth forms. I move so my tennis shoes are under me and try to stand without using my hands for support against the sharp grate. I grab for the handrail. The wee morning light causes the fog to glow, and I'm grateful I can see the railings. But this also means my time is running out. If the sun gets to its height before I reach mine, its rays will burn away the fog and my cover.

My skin is damp. My shoes are damp. I'm terrified I'll fall. I try to focus on my sister. Safe in her pajamas. Watching futilely from our shared bedroom window with the magnificent riverside view from our eighteenth-floor apartment.

I focus on Dad. Why I'm doing this. I imagine all the times he stood at that exact window with us, telling us stories from his work. Stories of history that they won't tell you in the classrooms anymore. Stories that would get our teachers fired if such tales spilled from their lips.

The real stories.

Ones with flags that dipped to half-staff during times of grief and loss. When loved ones lost lives en mass, the flags would lower for a few days, then rise up strong.

It gave people hope. A reason to continue. A reason to fight.

Especially people like Dad. Those risking their lives to save others.

I put one foot in front of the other. Lift, step. Lift, step. Grip the rail. And before I know it, I'm on landing four, and I pause again to catch my breath. Close my eyes. Breathe in the moist air and swallow the acid building in my esophagus.

I resist the urge to curl back to fetal on this fourth landing. I hug the rail nearest the tower's stone.

Buena Vista Freestone, it is. Thanks to Mrs. Sailor in fourth grade and her obsession with our local landmark. She'd crammed us full of all manner of facts regarding spinning cables and load limits. But the most fascinating was the freestone. At one time, long before my time, the bricks and blocks of the bridge towers were deep browns and tans.

I can't remember the details much. Only that buena vista means "good view." Not that I have a view of anything now. And I doubt the families and residents on either side of the river have a view of anything but the fog.

I do remember my Dad's flaming temper when I'd brought home a D on Mrs. Sailor's bridge test. "They'll teach this ridiculousness but won't give accurate history on anything else. Won't instill a sense of patriotism or loyalty to fellow man or country. To show even the most granular amount of concern for other human life. But bridges? We'll nail that down cold." When Mom replied that the latter was their job as parents, he'd let his rage dissipate. That's when he'd started spending more time with Jill and me. At the bedroom window. Strolling the Riverwalk. Hiking the bridge.

Teaching. Training. Encouraging us to be, well, human.

I catch my breath against the freestone, cold and scratchy columns of rock holding the entire bridge in place. The cables and rumbling road depend on it. The flags above stand tall on it. This middle tower feels larger than my entire apartment building. Maybe it is. I can't remember the specs.

My hands are so wet now, I can't tell if it's from the fog-soaked rail or sweat. That nasty sweat when you're completely warm at the core, but the exposed skin is cool and damp. Bundling up and sweating in the snow has a similar effect.

But it's the fog. Fog heavy enough to warrant an emergency alert system warning as early as last night.

So as early as last night, I decided this morning was it. My trek to the middle tower. I glance down toward where I think the bridge meets my shore. I don't see reds or blues or whites piercing the low cloud. I don't hear any sirens, not close ones anyway. So Sis hasn't ratted me out yet, or Mom surely would've called in Dad's buddies. To come and remove his grieving daughter from the tower's metal staircase.

"And please don't charge Michelle with trespassing, or jumping the locked gate guarding the bottom of the stairs. She's overcome with grief." The excuse will go.

Grieving, likely. Overcome? Most definitely.

I tear myself away from the sturdy stone and venture back to the metal stairway and aim up once more. More steps. *Focus, Michelle. Just two more landings.*

Jill is watching, I can feel it. We're not twins, but so incredibly close that we know each other's thoughts and finish each other's sentences. Ever since she got diagnosed, when the labored breathing and wheezing and weakness overtook her, we became all the more connected. Mom had to take extra work. Dad's hours were impossible.

I became her caretaker. A sister/mom/nurse combo pack.

Cystic fibrosis sucks.

I helped her with an extra treatment just before I headed out this morning. To ward off the buildup of mucus and secretions that threaten to drown her every few hours when the symptoms flare. And the stress of losing Dad has definitely made her symptoms worse.

All the crying doesn't help, either.

"You're nuts. You'll fall."

"Dad would want this."

"You don't have to do this." Jill had pleaded with me not to come.

Not to venture onto the bridge. Not to jump the gate securing the bottom of the stairway. Not to scale to the tip-top of the middle tower. Where the flags blow tall and proud despite the tragedy that overtook our family weeks ago.

That had overtaken hundreds of families since.

Senseless tragedies, Dad would say.

People not being human anymore. More worried about the weight of a suspension cable than treating fellow man with any ounce of respect.

I think, looking back, that Dad had been careful not to share all the gory details he'd seen in his workdays. He spared his girls those innocence-robbing visuals. His stories were more of summaries. As we grew older, Jill and I filled in the blanks with images from the local news channel.

Mothers abandoning children. Dads with children in five states, leaving a wake of single moms and ungrounded offspring. Young men and women lost and hopeless, scared to ask for help, seeking revenge on strangers in office buildings and school playgrounds.

And at soccer practices.

We could always tell when Dad had been called to one of those scenes based on the news reports. Ones that had made enough of a stir to gather camera crews.

A few of Dad's calls ended up on nationwide networks.

Dad's last call did. At the soccer field.

But the flags didn't dip to half-staff for him.

They hadn't fallen to half-staff for over two years. For any of them. And not just on this bridge. All over town.

All over the nation.

People just—forgot.

"We've been in trouble for a long while. But when we forget to honor our fallen, well, that's another tragedy all to itself." He'd put his arm around Jill and me. We used to watch the workers scale this grated staircase through Dad's old Army binoculars we kept on the windowsill. A few times we watched as they lowered the flag. A few days later, someone would come raise it again.

And that symbol of rising from the depths of despair, the stripes and stars flipping and snapping in the breeze, strong and proud, had given us hope.

For Jill, especially.

She and Dad had a special bond. And we all thought we'd lose Jill way before any of the rest of our family. It's just the way things were. An unspoken knowing.

Hoping for a cure to rise from the depths of disease research and come out tall and proud, flapping and waving in the clear blue sky that there was hope.

I pause midway between the fourth and fifth landing. The breeze picks up and I grip the rail harder, flakes of paint giving up their hold on the rusting metal and sticking to my wet palms. Tears well up and spill over, mixing with the mist on my face. I'm terrified I'll be seen as the fog breaks. As the sun's rays, as welcome as the early morning warmth would be, would steam off the cloud and the breeze would blow the droplets away. Terrified someone would stop me before I get to that flag.

I can't feel seconds or minutes, and I dare not fish my phone out from the layers of jackets, lest I drop the thing in the river. I can't tell how long I've been on this open-aired stairway. I can't tell how long it's taking me to go from one landing to the next. The only gauge of time is the increase in traffic and the ever-so-faint early morning skyline peeking through the tip-top of the fog. I can see the lights. Barely. But they're there. I've got to move.

I reach landing five.

Again, I make the turn toward the final set of steps, refusing to allow fear to send me curling into the corner. I'm almost there. I turn back toward our apartment. Streetlamps and rectangle windows from that shore shine glowing pinpoints toward the bridge.

The traffic sends rumbles up the metal landings a little faster. The metal railings have less time to recover from waves of vibrations between the passing cars.

I can't hear the water sloshing.

I'm too high.

Too many cars. I must have frozen at some point, not just on landing three. Probably at more than one point. Time is slipping faster.

I reach the top and go to my knees, feeling the buena vista freestone through my jeans. The breeze blows the metal hooks and pulleys against the pole. I crawl that way, to the middle, to the pole, too afraid to stand all the way up.

I focus on Jill. I know she can see the top of the bridge now, because I can see the top half of our apartment building. We'd joked about me doing the Rocky Balboa thing once I reached the pole.

The chicken dance would be more appropriate.

But no way. I'm stuck here on my hands and knees. Crawling like a coward.

I reach the aluminum pole. I know the base of the tower's top is quite wide. Wide enough to drive a car over. But I'm terrified I'll tip over the edge. I grasp the pole, hand over hand, and draw myself to a standing position. I look up. The flag flits now and then in the gentle breeze. Mostly it drips condensed fog onto my head. Its tears mix with mine.

I try to wipe my eyes and nose on my shoulder, but that doesn't accomplish much.

I will my frozen wet fingers to start working loose the rope from the cleat. The rope is wound around it tightly, but it finally gives.

For the flagpole at the station where Dad works—worked—the cleat is covered with a lock box to keep people from messing with it. This one is free to the air. Because who in their right mind would scale the middle bridge tower to mess with this flag?

As I wrestle the cable from the cleat, I remember all the times Dad had me help him with the station's flag. He'd shown me all things etiquette. How to dispose of the worn-out ones, how to fold the ones to give to families of fallen officers for their service. How to lower to half-staff and then raise it high again for Memorial Day and for those days when massive tragedy struck the nation.

Jill was never well enough nor possessed the arm strength required to manage the cables. This was me and Dad. Our thing.

Dad and Jill had window time and stories and special late-night snacks Mom never knew about—or pretended she didn't know about.

Dad was partial to white powdered doughnuts. The tiny ones in the paper bags. He said it wasn't cliché that he liked these so well, because real cops only liked the expensive glaze-covered or jelly-filled doughnuts.

I almost laugh as I remember his rationalization. But the burn in my shoulders and upper arms stifles it. This massive flag is much heavier dripping wet with cloud, and it's a much larger flag than the one in front of the station by far.

Finally, the cable is back on the cleat. The stars and stripes flit and wave halfway down the aluminum staff. A proper position of reverence and respect for the lives lost—those of family members and the service members who responded without regard for their own lives. The metal bits cling and clang once more.

The fog's veil lifted further while I worked with the flag. I can see all the way to the roadway below. To the walkway that Dad and Jill and I traversed so many beautiful days. Him talking. Training. Teaching.

Encouraging us to be human.

I pick out our tiny rectangular window as I drop to the tower's top and lean against the base of the pole.

I can't see Jill, but I know she's there. Munching on a breakfast of white powdered doughnuts in memory of Dad, leaving sticky fingerprints of powdered sugar on the binoculars.

And by this time, Mom's called in Dad's buddies regarding his grieving daughter and her irrational behavior.

Good thing. I think I'm stuck.

I think I'll be forgiven once my story's been told. Once I tell the officers of the journey in the fog up the side of the freestone tower to lower to half-staff a flag that should've been lowered in solemn reverence and raised up tall in hope dozens of times over the last couple of years.

I pull my knees up to my chest again and blow into my sore, cold hands.

I think I'll stay put for now, listening to the traffic rumble below and the metal clasps clanking against the aluminum pole above my head.

And I'll enjoy the buena vista.

Fetch

The boy didn't have much of a chance for success in life. The harsh, stark prairie and even harsher reality of his disability left him and his parents little hope. But with the help of Gilly the horse, the boy finally finds a way to contribute to his community.

Something he's good at.

Fetching.

My hat's a slidin' off my head down over my eyes and my rear cheeks are twitching with that achy draw that means it's time for me to slide down outta Gilly's saddle and take a stretch and wipe the sweat. So I do that. Gilly gives a snort and nods her head. The ol' gal seems glad for me to be off her back, though I know my mare'd carry me to the end of the world, or at least to the canyon's edge out yonder from our little valley.

Gilly's good and mine, Pa said. The only thing I truly own save for my name and the gimp in my leg. And I guess my dented tin canteen. I own that.

Red rock dust cakes on my boots and wiggles its way into my shoes as me and Gilly saunter toward the brook. I need new ones, seein' as how the stitchin's wearin' out and the bottoms are wearin' thin. And I've grown so much my big toes push against the ends when I walk, but Gilly needs water and I need a stretch. And times like these is when I'm thankful for my gimp 'cause only my left foot hurts. The right's a little littler and a lot less feely. Mostly numb most of the time.

More and more grime and crud wiggle in. Least it's dirt and not scorpion babies sneaking 'round.

And I got a good deal of growin' left to do so Ma says no use spendin' good coin on not-done-yet feet.

I untie my canteen and finish it off to the last drop. The thin leather strap is doubled back and again and tripled up through the handles. Plenty of leather, longer than my whole body by four hands. I don't want to lose my canteen, so I used plenty of strap.

I sorta lean on Gilly as we go. Her gray and white hide reminds me of the storm clouds that speckle then grow bigger as they get together and decide to drop the rain. She'd acted just like those storms once. As fast as gray lightning flickin' alive the sky. But she's got a little gimp in her and that's why Pa said she'd make a good first for me since I do all this fetchin' for folks. She's a good gal, ol' Gill, and I like leanin' close as we go, feelin' the muscles ripple in her shoulder and down her side. I reach and scratch behind her ear and she snorts again and sorta leans into me real gentle like, though I know she doesn't need to lean. She's not that gimp.

It's just a sort of leanin' kind of day. She's a horse, but she's smart about people and kinda knows when things are happy fetches or sad fetches. Like she's hitched up to all my feels. She just knows.

I like the happy fetches. The kinds that start with "Hey, Boy. Go fetch the hen crates from farmer McMandle." Gilly pulled a little kiddie wagon and we fetched the hen crates and delivered chickens to the neighbors. Time we got back my ears screamed with all their squawkin' complaints. It was worse than Ma's quiltin' bee ladies crowdin' in our sittin' room on too many lazy Saturdays. Those days I always wished someone'd yell "Fetch!" But chickens were happy things anyways.

Then there was that "Hey, Boy! Go fetch Doc Banks. Jessica's havin' the babe!" So we ran, well Gilly ran, and I hung on till my hands ached and my fingers got all numb like my gimp foot as we fetched Doc then he took his own wagon the three miles to Jessica's and delivered that baby nice and good. That was fun and happy. That was two years ago. That baby's up and walkin' 'round and gettin' all covered in dust and grime just like my boots.

Me and Gilly reach the brook and I secure her reins so's they don't dip in the creek as she drinks. Water's low with rocks a pokin' up through the stream and the water jigs and glides around them. I 'magine the ripples sayin' "Scuse me, ma'am pardon me, sir" to the pebbles as the water lazes its way south.

I fill my tin canteen, drink it all even though I catch silt and grit in my teeth, but it's wet and that's all that matters. I dip it into the creek and let some of the ripples worm inside. Gilly'll keep it safe for me in her saddle until I need it again. She's good at watchin' over things, my Gill.

My almost-there tree's ready for me. It's lonely and leany and only has leaves when it good and feels like it. The roots grab to the bank and are as big 'round as my Pa's legs. I can't wrap my arms around this tree like I can the spindly ones dotting in clumps here and there in the valley.

Twisted branches hang and reach clean to the other side of the brook, and when Pa taught me the way to George Washington's, he showed me how to climb out on the lowest limb. We'd tooked off our boots and climbed out and sat on that big limb like a pew in church, only we was barefoot and stinky 'cause it wasn't near Saturday night bath time yet, and we let our toes play in the brook, the water saying "'Scuse me, pardon me" as it wiggled past our feet.

We did this climbing out to the pew branch and he'd teach me tree names that I couldn't remember and flower names that I couldn't remember—case I ever needed to pick a bouquet of sweet daisies—I think he called them daisies—for some pretty lass some day. He'd taught me about rattlers and canteens and scorpions and how to keep safe on my fetches. "Fetchin' can earn you respect and maybe a livin' if you barter just right." He patted my right leg that time. He knew I'd not be cut out for millin' or farmin' or much heavy stuff like my brothers.

But I was good for fetchin'.

And I liked it.

I take off my hat, its brim worn as thin as the threads in my boots in spots, and wipe my sweat again as I sit with my back against the tree's bumpy hide. I don't bother checkin' for scorps or rattles. The dirt's taken over where the grass was last month. Only stubborn rough blades are left, but mostly, it's bare dirt under my marker tree and nothin' could hide here if its slithery life depended on it. I kick off my boots and pretend I'm a doin' the toes-in-the-creek thing because I can't stay long to enjoy.

White wispy clouds like Pa's tobacco smoke float high in the blue. As they go, I pretend they're playin' tag with the gnarled branches and limbs above me. At least the sky doesn't match Gilly.

That'd made this even a more of a leanin' day.

I left my hat in my lap and crisscross my arms behind my head and let my brown shag dry up a bit with the breeze. Gilly's relaxin' and lookin' round at the Valley and her withers twitch real lazy like and her black tail flicks the flies from her hind end. She keeps that one front hoof sorta up and raised when she can. It's the one that aches her, but she don't complain much. We're havin' a peaceful sort of almost-there rest, even if this is a sad sort of fetch.

I lean my head back and let the rays dance over my face through the branches above for just a bit more. Give both our gimps a good rest. I think George Washington's the best carpenter 'round. Sometimes I fetch wheel spokes or chicken boxes or rockin' chair arms. That sorta thing. But lately seems like mostly he does caskets. 'Specially after that fever ripped through the valley last year. Me and Gilly did lots of fetchin' out this way then when dyin' was more commonplace than livin'. I take him the measurements and he delivers the finished boxes with his own wagon and 'normous black horse, Eugene.

Eugene's a good three hands higher than Gilly and a lot stronger. Eugene and George Washington match in girth and color. George Washington's arms seem as long and sturdy as the hitchin' post outside the mercantile. Their hides are the same color. Black as night and shiny, too. All my life I've never seen no other man that color in the Valley. Horses. But no man.

But other folks 'round, specially the ladies, seem scared of that color. Or maybe it's how big he is or how he don't say too much. Just nods and smiles real faint like. It don't bother me none, though, and so that's why folks send me to do most of their fetchin' from him.

They don't much care for his name, neither, but I can't figure it. Teach said George Washington was a great leader. Great man. Founding father and all and he must've been a strong man to be a General and to have a country built on his shoulders. That's what the Teach had said. A country on his shoulders. But some people got all messed up in their talk, fightin' back and forth how someone that color shouldn't have no name like George Washington. Or Abraham Lincoln, neither. But Gilly and I don't know nobody who got that name.

I figure if you gotta have a name, may as well have one that's as strong as you are. His momma musta known he'd grow up to be a big strong man with big strong hands and a kind heart and that's why she gave him a grand name.

I reckon my Ma knew when I came out that I'd not fit a name like George Washington or John Adams. I kinda got a gimp in me like Gilly. Maybe that's why Gilly and me are all connected up. We just know each other.

I wipe my hands good and hard on my britches and check my shirt pocket. Miss Lilly gave me a roll of lace this morning. I'd been out waterin' those chatty chickens and a wonderin' what they gossip about all day when she came up behind me. I startled. She looked awful. She'd walked the quarter mile up our lane all by herself. Wearin' her black dress for Sunday and not standin' up straight like usual. And I knew.

"Fetch, would you please?" And she handed it to me and I tucked it in my pocket and told her "Yes, ma'am, I'm so sorry." And me and Gilly took off right quick. Things like this don't wait and give no permission for toes in the creek.

I pull the lace out and check on it. I hope my sweat didn't get to it. I don't think it did. It seems dry. It's her only bit of lace left, and she'd like to have it back. It's yellow like butter cream and dainty as lacy things should be. I don't unroll the tiny wad, though. I want to keep it clean. It's so tiny and frilly that I hope George Washington's fingers don't fray it as he uses it to measure. He'll have to stretch it out.

That's how this works.

I tuck the lace back into the pocket, satisfied it's clean and tidy, set my hat on my head and tuck my too-big-feet into too-small boots —at least only the left one hurts, can't feel the right one—and I mount Gilly and head for George Washington's.

We pick up the pace, kicking up dust and grime behind us and feeling that sunny breeze in our faces. Almost not fair, I think as we go along. Feeling good sunshine on a sad fetch. Poor Miss Lilly. How her heart must pound with sadness. And that tiny one…

I try to not think on it much. But one can't help it.

George Washington's cabin is just in view. The barn's leany and so's his front porch. From the looks of it, you'd not know he's the best carpenter 'round. But he is.

I slow Gilly, let her ease up so she'll not have such a time on the way back with her hoof. She'll be carrying more weight—but not much more, the dainty lace isn't that long.

I see George Washington dumpin' a fresh bucket into the trough out front. He musta clocked me comin' round the bend and was a gettin' ready for us. He's always kind that way. He takes Gilly's reins from me, she snorts at him real soft and gives him a nod. She's only a horse, but she's good at knowin' the rotten folks from the good ones. He hitches her up and she drinks from the trough and rests her gimp.

I slide from her back and pull out the tiny wad. I'd like to smile at George Washington and chat about trees and millin' and the news from up north in the Valley, but it's not a chattin' kind of a fetch. Not today.

His big brown eyes get all glossy and he wipes his hands on his bibs before he takes the lace roll in his palm. He could hold ten of those rolls at a time in that hand of his and still have room for more. I shake that thought right out of my head. That's a bad thought.

I follow him to his leany barn, and out front he's got the sawhorses all set up a workin' on some other something. Boards of all lengths lay scattered among piles of nails and handsaws and such. Scraps layin' here and there in the dirt. Some piled neat. Some scattered in heaps. Looks like he's a makin' a cabinet or shelves of some sort.

That'll have to wait now as he readies the sawhorses and moves them closer to each other 'cause he and me already know this little bit of lace isn't going to be near as long as his cabinet. He digs around in the board piles, and a brown mouse goes a flyin' from his hidin' spot deep under the pile. George Washington finds a few small planks and lays them like railroad ties across the sawhorses.

His fingers tremble a bit—I'd never seen that happen to his strong hands before. He takes the end of the buttercream frill between his thumb and finger and hands me the end. Then my hand trembles. Poor Miss Lilly. I hurt so bad for her, that I swear I feel pain even in my gimpy right foot.

I hold my end gently as he unrolls the lace. I'd wondered about his big ol' hands and how they'd do with this small job.

They did just kindly, that's how. That buttercream lace nearly blends perfect with the color of the boards. Slow and respectful like, he used the markin' pencil that he always kept tucked behind his ear to mark off the boards. He and me real gentle like rolled that lace up before his tears and mine could mix and stain it all up. It's Miss Lilly's last bit of lace. She'd like it back.

He sees me a sniffin' and snot startin' and says, "Eugene could use a rub-down." I don't argue. I find the big, black stallion on the other side of the barn, just a hangin' out. I hear George Washington's hand saw whizz and zip through the boards with a sad sort of rhythm.

Back. Forth.

Back. Forth.

If only livin' were more commonplace than dyin'.

I pat and rub and lean on Eugene and feel sick all over with grief. I startle when the hammerin' starts, and the pounding jerks the tears right outta my eyes, but Eugene doesn't mind. I decide to lead him over to Gilly so's the two friends could have a visit.

It don't take long before George Washington brings 'round the tiny wooden box. He don't take no effort at all liftin' it, and Gilly doesn't give no regardin' to its weight as George Washington straps the thing to the back of her saddle. I've got plenty of room for the ride home. Eugene rubs his shoulder against Gilly's and heads to the side of the barn, head droopin' low. Even the grand Eugene's sensitive enough to pick up on this sad fetch.

Eugene's probably all hitched up to George Washington's feels like Gilly's hitched up to mine.

I reach my hand to shake the deal done. No coin needed. He'd only used bits of scraps for this casket. His black face, shiny with streaks of sweat and tears through the dust said enough. George Washington's kind that way.

He unhitches my mare as I climb into her saddle. Gilly and I nod our thanks and we head north, leaving George Washington slumped on his leany front porch with his head in his massive, kind hands.

My feet hurt deep in my boots. Both my feet. And the sweat's a comin' a little faster, though the sun's dipped a little lower and this shouldn't be the case. I see my almost-there-tree and the brook and decide I'll have to stop and drink and stretch.

I tie back Gilly's reins so they don't get wet while she drinks. I drink all my canteen up and give it back to her for safe keepin'. Then I rest under the tree again while she twitches and rests her own foot.

My eyes want to force shut and I'm outta breath but I manage to slide outta my boots. My right foot's all swollen and shines brilliant red like the growing sunset where pale peach used to be. It hurts, but only barely. And for that I'm grateful.

I wonder if that little brown mouse was the only critter hidin' in George Washington's pile of boards.

My hat's a slidin' off my head and my whole being has that achy draw that means it's time to take a long rest. My almost-there-tree supports my back with its bumpy hide. I can't remember what kind of tree this is.

Pa would know.

The brook ripples and gurgles beside us, making its apologies to the rocks and stones on its way south. I check my pocket for Miss Lilly's lace. I put my hand over my pocket to keep it safe. It's her last bit and she'll want it back.

I let my hat slide down over my face after one last glance at the sun and my trusty mare. Gilly'll watch over the tiny casket. She'll steady herself over me, casting a strong shade so the last part's not so bad—she's all hooked up to my feels, and I know she knows. Her saddle holds my canteen with the leather strap all doubled and tripled back on itself, longer than me, so there'll be plenty to measure.

That's my lace. That strap.

And then someone will fetch George Washington for me, and he'll have to adjust those sawhorses all over again.

Wouldn't You Like to be a
Red-Winged Blackbird?

Spring blooms again, and a fresh year dawns. For Max, the new and the old form a bittersweet blend as she takes to the old country roads with her camera to find the ever-elusive red-winged blackbird.

The snow melted slowly, leaving blotchy patches of white in the yard and along the ditches. Green grass struggled to find its breath, and the noise of happy spring birds returned. Max grabbed her Nikon and ventured outside. It was early, but hearing the chirps outside her window this afternoon sparked Max into action. She'd been editing photos for her show far too long and needed to stretch.

She hung the camera around her neck and took in the sweet smell of fresh spring. She loved working from home. And home was five miles from the nearest neighbor in all directions. A wooded ravine bordered her property on one side, farmland bordered the others. She wished Marie could take part in the springtime contest like she did when they were children.

She started down the country road, her boots clacking gently on the pavement. Max smiled as she remembered a similar stretch of country road that separated her house from her best friend's. About a half mile stretch with a couple of curves. The girls had worn out a path to the side of the ditch running back and forth.

A sparrow lighted atop a rugged fence post and Max raised the Nikon, but the creature took flight before she could get the shot. She let the camera fall to her chest and kept walking.

Max's mother had thought up the contest one spring afternoon when she and Marie had broken the table lamp while trying to pitch a tent indoors with blankets and jump ropes. Mom had had enough and figured she'd be money ahead with ten one-dollar bills and a brand new game if the girls just went outside. A few years later, Marie would tell Max that her mom must be a genius to be able to come up with something so grand.

The rules had been simple. Each girl started with five dollars. The first one to spot a robin earned a dollar from the other girl. The first one to spy a rainbow—and not one from the garden hose, but a God-given rainbow in the sky—earned a dollar from the other one. Same thing for the first butterfly, toadstool and wildflower.

The girls' eyes had bugged and their jaws dropped as they counted their money.

"Well, get on now. You can't find these things sitting in here."

"But what if we can't find all these today? What then?" Marie asked.

Mom smiled and said, "It may take you more than one day. Especially the rainbow. That one might be difficult."

"What if she finds something when I'm not around? How will I know she's not fibbin'?"

"Marie, does your mom have a Polaroid?" Marie nodded as she laid her dollars out side by side on the old kitchen table.

"Well, if you're apart, you'll have to take a photo and put a date on it and then settle up later." She brushed the stringy brown hair from Max's face. "My camera's in the closet. You're welcome to use it, but just for the game, okay?"

Max nodded. Marie squealed and the girls were off. They'd been six years old.

Max looked down at her Nikon with all the bells and whistles of modern digital photography. She wished she still had Mom's old Polaroid. She wished she still had a lot of things.

A tractor rumbled toward her, and she hopped over the ditch to allow it room to pass. Dave waved down to her and she waved back. She aimed the camera at the rear of the tractor and caught a decent stylistic shot. She'd have to edit out the telephone lines and blur out the license plate. The shot would be a perfect fit for the photography scholarship fundraiser in New York this weekend.

She continued, looking for that first robin. That first wildflower. Anything from the list that she could add to her personal gallery wall.

The gallery had been Marie's idea, about five years into the game. In Marie's basement, her parents allowed her to hang framed photos from that spring's contest. Purple frames represented Max's wins, and pink frames represented Marie's.

The girls bored of the original list after the first couple of years, so they added items of their own. First tree bud. First dragonfly. First strawberry.

The caveat, at that point, was they'd have to fund anything above five dollars each with their own money. Mom wasn't about to fund a list of one hundred items. And the thing was, it wasn't even about the money. They did it for the thrill, and each season the girls ended up even anyway.

By the time they were twelve, it was all about the photos.

Each girl asked for nicer cameras for birthdays and extra rolls of film for their Christmas stockings. Each year, their parents obliged. The pair were even elected as school photographers in sixth grade, attending ball games and award ceremonies for the school. They sent their photos to the local newspaper for a dollar apiece. Those dollars helped fund the next hunt.

A passing car with dual exhaust startled Max from her thoughts. After the gush of wind and dust that followed the intrusion settled, she decided to cross the fence line—Dave told her she could do so any time so long as it was before the field was planted—and sit with her side against one of the posts. The ground was cold and damp, and soaked her jeans, but the perfect shot was worth a little discomfort.

From her view on the ground, she could focus the Nikon on the long, rugged fence line and hope for another bird shot. Hopefully, a red-winged blackbird. She didn't want to settle for a robin.

When the girls reached middle school, their list had become so specific that Max lost track of who'd added which species. The robin was still on the list, but the girls had added ten other birds along with Queen Anne's Lace and Sweet Rocket wildflowers that lined the ditches of their Midwest home.

The red-winged blackbird was Marie's favorite. Max would never forget that conversation.

"Wouldn't you like to be one?" Marie asked one day as they picked up their developed film from the drug store down the road from the school.

"Be one what?" Max was flipping through the photos of the basketball tournament to find the nature shots she'd taken earlier that week.

"Wouldn't you like to be a red-winged blackbird?" Marie handed Max a shot of the bird she'd taken two days ago—with one shot left on her roll of thirty-five millimeter. Max was shocked. It took her five or six tries with the birds before she got a photo that good.

"Wow, that's amazing!" The bird had landed on the school's stone nameplate at the front entrance. Marie hadn't gotten any of the lettering in the shot, and the background was blurred enough so you couldn't easily tell where it was taken. The bird's ebony feathers had a slight purple sheen, and its shoulder boasted a scarlet patch trimmed with a slender line of bright white.

"I'd like to be one for a day. To fly. I know the girl ones are brown and dull, but I'd like to fly and have that fiery red flame come from my shoulders." Marie gazed at the photo and tucked it back into her packet.

"You should send that one in."

Marie grinned and nodded. "I think I might."

Their photos became more and more impressive and both girls entered and won junior photography contests. Marie's red-winged took grand prize at the state fair. Sleek black and silver frames gradually replaced the pinks and purples in Marie's basement, and only the best of the best made it onto the wall.

Max adjusted her position and held up the camera toward the fence line as a bird, too far away to identify, floated in the breeze above her head. Sitting this still on the ground was always a challenge, and with age, it was becoming more of one.

She fought back tears, not from the pain in her lower back, but from the emptiness in her heart as she remembered that last spring with Marie.

The girls had been at Max's house in the back yard, taking photographs of the beige toadstools that popped up near the pine trees each spring. Marie spotted them first, but both took different shots. Different angles. Different lighting. Lying smack on the ground, noses and camera lenses inches from the fungus.

Marie rolled over on her back in the grass after the photo shoot.

Max mirrored her, their heads together, looking up at the graying sky to the west.

"Betcha there'll be a rainbow soon."

"Maybe. Not much light left though, and I've gotta get home

soon to study for that dumb history quiz." Marie sat up, and put her camera back into its case.

"Okay. See ya tomorrow." Max remained in the grass, watching the clouds.

Marie stood and brushed off her jeans. "See ya."

That was the last time the girls spoke.

The bird swooping above Max's head was a crow. That figures. Sometimes you see what you want to see. But the camera never lies. She swung around to face the opposite direction. The light was better from that angle and her right shoulder was numb from the post and needed a break.

From this vantage point, Max had the wooded area near her home in the frame, and a few fence posts. Several more birds of varying sizes were still too far off to capture or identify. She held up her camera, waited patiently, and allowed anniversary memories to sweep over her.

Max had walked in the back door when her mom called her out the front door. Max sat her camera down and went through the house to the porch. It had started to sprinkle, and Max thought about retrieving her camera to catch that rogue rainbow, but something in her mom's voice gave her pause.

Mom pointed down the road to the curve about an eighth of a mile past their house. The blind curve that the girls had been warned about since they were little. The curve that caused them to walk in the ditch, wearing out that path between their homes. The curve that all the locals knew to approach with caution. And most of them knew that the two little girls frequented that part of the road.

A couple of cars had stopped, and the people were exiting their vehicles. Max took off running. Rain fell a little harder, soaking her shoulders.

A white pickup truck was off in the ditch, rear passenger tire still spinning slowly in mid-air.

She saw Marie's camera, out of the case, busted on the pavement. Then, around the bend in the road, she saw Marie's boots, then her legs, then her whole form.

Max fell to the road next to her friend in the pouring rain.

"I didn't see her. I just didn't see her. She was right there in the middle…" The driver was babbling and disoriented.

Marie didn't move. Max laid her head on Marie's chest and couldn't hear a heartbeat. She couldn't feel her chest rise and fall.

Max stayed in that position until her mother pulled her away so Marie's parents could come near. Max stumbled backward to the middle of the road and cried up to the sky. The rain had slowed and the evening sunlight cast just the right angle…

And then Max knew.

From the middle of the road, in the middle of the blind spot, was the perfect shot. Framed by trees on each side. No power lines. Perfect light.

Marie had found spring's first rainbow.

MAX GAVE UP THE WAIT. She had several more hours of editing for the show this weekend. She stood slowly, letting the cramps work out of her legs and back. She stepped over the ditch and onto the road when something fluttered in the corner of her eye. On the post she had leaned against for the last hour was a perfect, glossy red-winged blackbird.

Slowly the Nikon came up to her face. Slowly she focused. Slowly she moved her finger to the shutter release.

A gallery-worthy photo.

A Marie Hawkins Photography Scholarship piece.

And she got it with one click.

About the Author

Beth enjoys chucking words into sentences then standing back to see what magic—or mayhem—falls out, crafting tales in mystery, sci-fi, fantasy, and general "slice of life" fiction. She couldn't accomplish this without the help of her tutu-clad Little Miss Muse and Trudi the Concrete Office Goose, who's partial to superhero capes.

Her stories have appeared in multiple publications, including Pulphouse Fiction Magazine and Ellery Queen Mystery Magazine, and in multiple fiction anthologies. She's received several Honorable Mentions from Writers of the Future. Her lighthearted blog peeks into the writing life as she pokes fun at herself and her circus of a life.

Follow the antics of Little Miss Muse and Trudi, read Beth's blog (she might have burned down her kitchen last week), and discover the stories at bapaul.com.

Also by B. A. Paul

Short Story Collections

Spunk and Spice, Volumes 1 and 2: A Collection of six short stories celebrating timeless wit and wisdom.

Out There, Volumes 1 and 2: A Collection of six short sci-fi and speculative tales.

Mystery Minutes, Volumes 1 and 2: Six short mystery stories

All the Feels, Volumes 1, 2, and 3: Collections of inspiring short stories

Just a Tick of Whimsy, Volumes 1 and 2: Collections of fantasy shorts.

Hijacked Holidays: Definitely not your warm-and-fuzzy winter tales.

Dark Minds: Toe-curling twisted mysteries.

Blog Compilations: Slices of the writing life with lots of laughs and bumps in the road.

Life Along the Way

Life All Over Again

Novels

Triage

Young Adult (or Young at Heart) Books

Switch: Book 1 in the Oliver Andrews Trilogy

BAPAUL.COM

Take a glimpse into B.A. Paul's writing journey, including the ups and downs of managing family, "real jobs," ducks in wobbling rows, and chasing down her Little Miss Muse. New blog posts go up Mondays, with the first Monday of the month reserved for a free fiction short story available on the blog for a limited time.

Newsletter Signup!

Get the latest release information, author updates, and exclusive content by signing up at bapaul.com.